## A Fairy Houses Mystery (#2)

www.fairyhouses.com

## A Fairy Houses Mystery (#2)

### by

## Tracy Kane &
## Genevieve Aichele

Light-Beams
PUBLISHING
www.light-beams.com

Author/Illustrator: Tracy Kane
Author: Genevieve Aichele
Design: Barry Kane
Art Director/Design: Tracy Kane

Publisher's Cataloging-In-Publication Data
(Prepared by The Donohue Group, Inc.)

Kane, Tracy L.
   Ocean secrets / by Tracy Kane and Genevieve Aichele.

     p. : ill. ; cm. ~ (A fairy houses mystery ; #2)

   Summary: Exploring the Isles of Shoals, Kate and Luke discover the magic along these rocky shores, including what looks like an underwater fairy castle in a tidal pool. Also, out at sea, pirates, ghosts, and a feisty seal are just the beginning of a secret new world of adventure awaiting them.
   Interest age level: 007-011.
   Issued also as an ebook.
   ISBN: 978-0-9766289-5-8 (hardcover)
   ISBN: 978-0-9766289-6-5 (softcover)

   1. Fairies~Juvenile fiction. 2. Ocean~Juvenile fiction. 3. Friendship~Juvenile fiction. 4. Fairies~Fiction. 5. Ocean~Fiction. 6. Friendship~Fiction. 7. Mystery and detective stories. I. Aichele, Genevieve. II. Title. III. Series: Fairy houses series ; #2.

PZ7.K12757 Oce 2014
[Fic]

18 17 16 15 14   6 5 4 3 2 1

Printed in Hong Kong.

Light-Beams Publishing
www.light-beams.com

*For everyone who enjoys and protects*
*Nature's wonders.*

T. K.


*For Aylin, Emel, Brynn & Oliver*

G. A.

Special thanks to Dana Rau, Kara Steere
and Patricia Day Aichele

Thanks to Cornell University and
The New Hampshire Department of Forestry
for saving Creek Farm for all to enjoy.

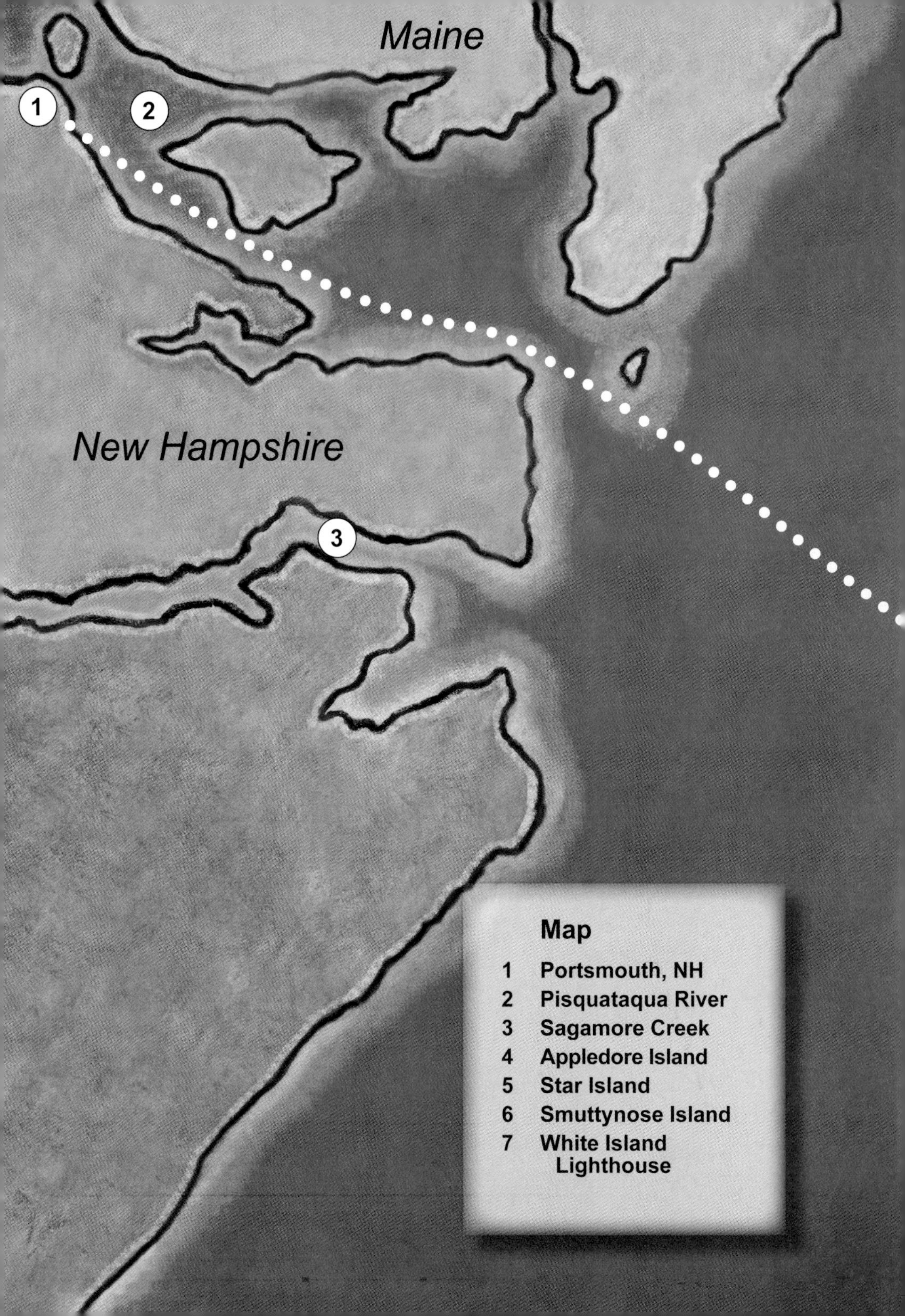

Maine

New Hampshire

**Map**

1   Portsmouth, NH
2   Pisquataqua River
3   Sagamore Creek
4   Appledore Island
5   Star Island
6   Smuttynose Island
7   White Island
    Lighthouse

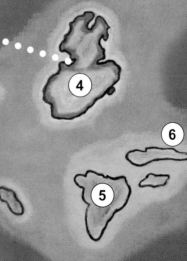

Atlantic Ocean

*Isles of Shoals*

## Chapter ONE

In the bright October sunlight, sparkles danced across the waters of Sagamore Creek near Portsmouth, New Hampshire. It was low tide, and the wet sand glittered from the water's edge to where a small triangular shape rose two feet from the ground. It looked like a rustic teepee, and was constructed from pieces of driftwood, sand and stones.

Circling above, a curious seagull spotted movement at the base of the structure and flew in close, hoping for a tasty snack. Then he noticed three humans approaching the shoreline. He screeched a warning at them and headed toward the ocean instead.

The three figures were two older children and a smaller girl, who dragged her brother by the hand and urged him toward the teepee.

"Wow! This fairy house is really amazing, Meg," Luke said. "It's clever how you used the driftwood and rocks to help make it strong."

1

"Do you like it, Kate?" Meg asked the older girl.

"I love how you decorated it with the seashells and seaweed," Kate said. "Did you make this all by yourself?"

"I had a little help from Mrs. Lennox," Meg answered. "She said even old ladies like to make fairy houses, and I can build them on her land anytime I want."

"Mrs. Lennox said Luke and I could explore her property whenever we wished," Kate said. "It's like having your own private woods with a seaside park. Look, you can even see her mansion from here."

They all looked up the knoll to where a large white house commanded a view of the water. Behind it as far as you could see was a forest of trees.

"Maybe her house wouldn't look so old and spooky if it had a new coat of paint," Luke said.

"I think it looks romantic, looking over the water with that great porch and all those windows," Kate said. "My mom says there's no other house quite like it in Portsmouth and it should be—"

A loud horn interrupted Kate as a lobster boat motored past them on the far side of the creek.

"Hey!" shouted Luke as he and Meg waved to the man at the helm. "That's Dad going to the harbor to check on his lobster pots again."

"How many times do you have to check the traps to see if there are any lobsters?" Kate asked.

"Normally, a couple times a week," Luke said, "but recently somebody has been stealing the lobsters and sometimes their cages, too. Dad and the other lobstermen are taking turns patrolling the area, hoping to find who's doing it."

"Look!" Meg said. "A fairy has been visiting my house."

"How do you know?" Kate asked.

"The berries I left in the mussel shell for the fairies to eat are all gone," Meg replied.

Kate looked up and caught Luke winking at her. "Meg," he asked, "what's that little hole in the floor of your house?"

Meg leaned in closer. "I think I see something," she said. Suddenly she jumped up and bumped into Kate as a small crab scuttled sideways out of the hole and into some nearby rocks. Disappointed, Meg tugged at her dark brown ponytail. "I thought it might have been a fairy."

"But isn't it great that a crab likes your house?" Kate asked. "You know, animals are friends of the fairies."

Hoping to cheer up his five-year-old sister, Luke squatted down and began skittering sideways across the beach with his hands opening and closing like claws.

"What are you doing?" Meg giggled.

"The Crabby Shuffle—it's the new dance craze!"

Soon they were all spinning and dancing around the fairy house. Even though Luke and Kate were already in sixth grade, they both loved nature's wonders and never grew tired of having fun outdoors. Kate's straight reddish-brown hair flew in her face as she landed, laughing on the sand. Near her hand, she noticed a pile of pebbles. "Look," she said, holding one up. "This is a lucky stone! It has a light ring running all around it."

"You mean lucky like a four-leaf clover?" Luke asked.

"Yes. See that?" Kate pointed to the ring of white zigzagging around the pebble.

"Let's find some more for my fairy house!" Meg said.

Together, they found a handful of stones and placed them in a circle next to Meg's fairy house.

Kate announced, "This is a fairy ring where the fairies dance on a moonlit night."

"Really?" Meg asked. "Do you think the fairies dance the Crabby Shuffle?"

# Chapter TWO

"I want to tell Mrs. Lennox about the crab and the lucky stones," Meg said. They all headed up the path toward Mrs. Lennox's house. Kate and Luke had been afraid of their older neighbor last summer. But when Mrs. Lennox discovered them building fairy houses, it reminded her how she had built them herself when she was eleven. Now, Kate and Luke were invited to create fairy houses on the Lennox property whenever they wished, and all three were friends.

As they passed a large oak tree, Kate said, "Oh look, there are the fairy houses I built with two of my new friends at school. There were lots of natural things to use, especially pinecones and acorns this time of year."

"I didn't know you brought other kids from our class out here," Luke said.

Kate noticed that Luke looked a bit rejected. "You were working with your Uncle Rick that day," she said.

"I could have showed them how to build some amazing gnome homes," Luke said.

"What's a 'nowm'?" asked Meg.

Just then, the children heard a rustling sound. On the path at the edge of Mrs. Lennox's lawn, seven waxwing birds were lined up on the branch of a mountain ash tree. Luke, Kate and Meg watched as one bird used its beak to pluck a bright orange berry and pass it along to the next bird. That waxwing passed the berry to the third bird, and the berry continued down the line until the last bird gobbled it up.

"Wow," Luke said. "My Uncle Rick says waxwings sometimes feed each other this way, but I've never seen it before—and with so many. I wish I had my camera with me. This would make a great photo."

"They're forming groups and migrating south for the winter," Kate said. "Remember last month when the monarch butterflies were gathering in large orange clouds and heading south along the coastline?"

"Sure I do," Luke replied. "Remember that close-up picture I took of them when they landed on my boat?"

"Monarch butterflies fly all the way to Mexico," Kate said. "I think some of them slept in our fairy houses on their way."

"Luke, would you take a picture of my fairy house?" Meg asked.

Suddenly, a squirrel landed in the tree and all the waxwings took flight.

Meg gathered a handful of the orange berries that had scattered on the ground. "Can I put these on my fairy house?"

"Maybe tomorrow," Luke replied, "and I'll take a photo of you next to your fairy house."

"Luke, listen!" Kate said. "Do you hear that? It's music coming from Mrs. Lennox's house."

They all stopped and listened as the tinkling of a piano drifted through the trees. The sound seemed to be coming from the west wing of the house.

"Come on," Luke said. "We need to investigate."

# Chapter THREE

As they approached the side of the house, the children could see a large door standing open. As long as Luke could remember, this wing of the house had been empty, the doors locked and some of the window shutters nailed closed. The setting sun illuminated a magnificent spider web in the doorway with its maker sitting in the center. Obviously, the door hadn't been opened in a long time.

Inside, Annie Lennox was dancing to the music and humming. Her silver hair shimmered as she glided through the dusty sunbeams streaming from the west window. She was wearing colors that reminded Kate of sea glass— soft muted greens and blues. The chiffon scarf she wore followed her movements like an ocean wave.

"Mrs. Lennox looks like one of the fairy godmothers in Sleeping Beauty," whispered Kate, not wanting to surprise the dancing woman. "You'd never guess she is in her late seventies."

The three children watched her move around the large, ancient room with its tall ceiling and dark rafters. Mrs. Lennox's slow but elegant moves were followed by a few quick sidesteps.

"She's doing the Crabby Shuffle!" Meg giggled.

Startled, the older woman stopped at the sound of Meg's voice and turned quickly to see the three shadowed figures in the doorway.

"Oh! It's just you three," Mrs. Lennox sighed in relief as she turned off the music.

"Is that a waltz?" Kate asked.

"Not really," Mrs. Lennox replied. "I just invent steps as I go along. I'm a bit rusty … I haven't danced in ages. But today I'm celebrating."

"Is it your birthday?" Luke asked.

"Certainly not!" Mrs. Lennox laughed. "I stopped celebrating birthdays a while ago. No, today I received the good news that the New Hampshire Department of Forestry is going to take over my land."

"And keep it just the way it is?" Kate asked.

"Yes! Isn't that wonderful?" Mrs. Lennox said.

Then her smile faded a bit. "It would be the perfect solution except for one problem. They don't want the house. They say it's too big and needs too much work, and they don't have the money to fix it up and care for it."

Kate looked around the room, with its impressive wood ceiling. An enormous painting of children playing in the woods hung over a large, stone fireplace. "This place is so amazing," she said. "It could be a museum."

"That painting must be really old," Luke said. "Did kids not wear clothes back then?"

Mrs. Lennox laughed. "That's the way children were often painted in the late 1800s, innocent and natural in the outdoors."

"You know, the boy with the dark, curly hair reminds me of you, Luke," Kate said with a smile.

Luke quickly changed the subject. "So what will happen to the house, Mrs. Lennox?"

"I'm afraid it might have to be destroyed," Mrs. Lennox said sadly. "I was upset about it at first but have decided it's probably for the best. At least this beautiful land will be saved, and that's the most important thing to me."

"Why can't the house be repaired?" Kate asked. "People like to save old houses in New Hampshire."

"Destroy the house! That can't happen!" said a silhouette from the doorway. Kate recognized her mother's familiar voice.

"This house is an amazing building and so unique. We have to find some way to preserve it." Kerry Evans walked briskly around the room, her blond hair light against the dark walls. "Look at this magnificent place! I wish the walls could talk—I'm sure they could tell us some entertaining stories."

"This space was designed to be a music room by the original owner back in the early 1900s," Mrs. Lennox said. "The acoustics are wonderful. Do you notice how clear our voices are? Friends would gather here, play music and give performances. Poets like Celia Thaxter would recite. That was how people entertained themselves back before television."

"You work at Strawbery Banke Museum, Mom. Maybe they can buy it," Kate said.

"I'm afraid they have enough historical buildings to keep up right now," her mother replied.

"Mrs. Lennox, will you tell me the story again about your mother and her sister and brother who built the fairy houses here when they were little?" Meg asked.

"Maybe another time, Meg," Mrs. Evans said. "Your mother just called, and she needs you and Luke home for dinner. It gets dark so early in October. I could give you a ride home if you like."

"It's not far, Mrs. Evans, but thank you," Luke said as he and Meg ducked under the spider web and headed out.

"Come on, Kate," said her mom. "I've got dinner waiting, too."

"I bet you invited Luke's Uncle Rick to join us," Kate said. "You seem to be seeing a lot of him lately."

"It's been for business mostly," said her mom shyly.

"Don't worry, Mom," Kate said. "I like Rick. You've been alone for a long time since Dad died."

"Would you like to join us, Annie?" her mom asked. "You can tell Rick the good news about your property. After dinner, it would be wonderful to hear about what it was like when you were Kate's age living at Creek Farm."

"I would enjoy that," Mrs. Lennox said. "Let me get my coat, and then I'll waltz my way over with you!"

# Chapter FOUR

After school, Luke headed to Prescott Park to find his uncle, who was the head gardener there. Luke found Rick Fernandez putting away gardening tools in the old warehouse that stuck out over the Piscataqua River.

Pulling off his cap to wipe his brow, Rick said, "It's been an unusually hot October this year." His dark wavy hair looked just like Luke's, which wasn't surprising since Luke's mom is Rick's twin sister.

Luke liked the view from the warehouse of the tidal river that was the border between New Hampshire and Maine. There were always lobster and fishing boats to watch as well as sailboats and kayaks. Sometimes even a submarine would come in to be repaired at the Navy Yard over on the Maine side. But Luke's favorite boats were the barges that needed the tugboats to guide them in. The barges were so large that when they came into or left port, two bridges had to be raised. All the cars traveling between the two states had to wait until the giant ships passed through.

"Uncle Rick," Luke said, turning from the window, "Dad told me this morning that we're all going to the Isles of Shoals for Columbus Day weekend. Four whole days! I've only been near the islands on Dad's lobster boat. I've never had a chance to explore them or spend the night out there and—"

"Slow down there, Luke. It's not just a vacation, you know," Uncle Rick said. "There is work to do at the Cornell Marine Lab on Appledore Island. Your dad and I have been hired to make sure everything is properly shut down and closed up for the winter. I've also invited Kate and her mom to come along. Everyone going out there is expected to pitch in—even Meg."

"And who is Meg?" asked a tall, lanky figure in the doorway.

Luke looked up at an older boy with straight, blond hair and a slim face. He was wearing a red sweater, and Luke thought he must be around sixteen years old.

"Luke," Rick said, "this is Ian Darby. Ian's dad is an ornithology professor who teaches college students at the marine lab. Ian, this is my nephew Luke Carver. Meg is his younger sister. The whole family is coming to help us close up."

"So what does an orna...orna...ornacollegy professor do?" Luke asked.

"Birds, my friend. An ornithologist studies birds!" Ian laughed. "I've been going out to Appledore Island with my dad every summer for years. Now that I'm older, I've even been helping him catch and tag the birds."

"Ian knows the ropes out there, and he stayed to help us close up before he flies home to England," Uncle Rick explained. "He'll be staying at Annie's house until we head out on Friday."

"Great," Luke said. "That's only in three days. I can't wait to tell Kate."

"I gather Kate isn't your older sister, Luke," Ian said. "Perhaps she's your girlfriend?"

"She's just a friend," Luke replied, as he felt his face turning the color of Ian's sweater. Why did older boys always feel they had to be so clever?

"We leave at sunrise," Uncle Rick said. "The ocean should be calm then, and the high tide will be perfect for a boatload of people. Now, will you two please carry these boxes to the end of the pier? They have the tools and supplies we need to take with us. Luke, your dad will be picking them up later after he checks his lobster pots."

Ian and Luke each grabbed a box and headed out in silence. Along the pier, the dock posts lined up like soldiers. The top of each post was claimed by a cormorant. Some of the birds held their black wings out to dry in the breeze. Suddenly, one cormorant dove like an arrow into the water. In moments, he resurfaced with the tail of a fish sticking out from his bill. The bird's neck had expanded, and he struggled for a moment to swallow his large meal.

"It's amazing how much they can swallow in one go," Luke said, breaking the silence. "Cormorants can dive really deep to catch fish, and their ancestors have been traced way back to when dinosaurs lived."

"Have you ever heard how the fishermen in

Asia used to train cormorants to fish for them?"
Ian asked. When Luke shook his head, Ian
continued. "They would tie a snare near the
base of the bird's throat so the cormorant could
only swallow small fish. If the bird caught a big
fish, part of it would stick out of its mouth and
the fisherman would pull it out for himself."

"Is that true?" Luke asked suspiciously.

"Look, I've spent my summers on the islands

with college students who study the ocean, and all the animals and plants that live off it," Ian said. "I'm a sixteen-year-old walking encyclopedia of ocean trivia."

"I wonder if I could take some classes out there in a couple of years," Luke said.

"Well, if you do, then I'm the one to show you around," Ian replied with a secret smile.

# Chapter
# FIVE

"The stars seem brighter tonight," Kate said
as she put the large pumpkin in the wheelbarrow
Luke had found in Mrs. Lennox's garden shed.

"I never thought about using a pumpkin for
a fairy house," Luke said. "It's clever the way you
carved a door and windows into it."

Kate beamed as Luke helped her lift the
pumpkin fairy house onto the porch. "Mrs.
Lennox," she called. "Come look!"

Mrs. Lennox was delighted. "Shall we put
a candle inside? I have one right here on the
porch."

She lit the candle, and they all admired the
effect of the soft, orange glow.

"Now it looks like someone is living there,"
Kate said.

"What, is it Halloween already?" Ian said as
he came onto the porch. "Is that a house for
hobbits? You Americans sure know how to do
up holidays."

"No, it's a fairy house," Kate replied, looking

up at the tall youth with the striking blue eyes. "You must be Ian. My name's Kate."

"Glad to meet you, Kate," Ian said. "Are you the creator of this pumpkin house? I don't know about fairies, but I could see a mouse taking up residence in it. You aren't afraid of mice are you? I have a sister your age in England who would take off running if she saw even a little mouse."

"I think mice are cute," Kate said. "I'd be happy if one decided to make my fairy house its home."

"Mrs. Lennox," Luke asked, "didn't you say Kate and I could go up to see the clock tower in the attic tonight?"

"Certainly, but take a flashlight," Mrs. Lennox said. "It's dark up there, and I'm not sure the attic lights are working. You better go with them, Ian."

"Brilliant, I'd love to see the clock tower," Ian said.

As the three of them headed up the steep stairs to the attic, Ian raved about the architecture of Mrs. Lennox's house and how special it was. "Talk about fairy houses, this place is like a giant fairy house."

Luke opened the door to the attic and shone the flashlight around the dusty room. Something flew out of the darkness, brushed past Luke's face and then almost got caught in Kate's hair before flying up to the rafters.

"Whaaaat wwwass that?" Luke asked, dropping the flashlight. The beam of light bounced around the attic walls before it settled to the floor.

"I think it was a bat," Kate said, as she quickly brushed her hair with her hand. "I wonder how it got inside."

"You don't seem too upset," Ian looked at Kate with admiration as he bent over to pick up the flashlight. He handed it to Luke and flashed him a sly smile. "Most of the girls I know would be screaming by now."

Not waiting for the answer, Luke continued into the attic. He moved the flashlight around until the beam landed on what he was searching for. "Look!" he said. "Here's the clock. This is the backside of it, and you can see all the workings. The gears look rusty, and that's

probably why it has stopped keeping time. Maybe a little oil could fix it." Luke paused, then added, "But I suppose it doesn't matter now if the whole house is going to be torn down."

"This house?" Ian asked. "Who would want to tear this house down?"

"Mrs. Lennox is leaving her land to the New Hampshire Department of Forestry," Kate explained. "They don't need the house, and if we don't find someone who does, it will be torn down."

"That would be a shame," Ian said. "With this spooky clock tower and bats in the belfry, tourists would pay money to tour this haunted mansion. Let me think about this. I have a reputation for coming up with great ideas."

# Chapter SIX

Luke skillfully navigated his small skiff alongside the dock at Wilson's boatyard, and Ian hopped out. "Thanks for dropping me, mates," he called to Kate and Luke. "As soon as the repairs are finished, I'll bring the lab boat to the Prescott Park dock."

Luke waved goodbye, turned the skiff and headed back across the river. "Let's troll for fish on our way back," he said. He set out a baited line for Kate to drag behind while he slowly guided his boat to the opening where Sagamore Creek joined the Piscataqua River. As they dodged lobster buoys, Luke told Kate what his father had said about the lobster thefts.

"For the past three months," Luke shouted over the sound of the boat's motor, "someone has been stealing lobsters along the New England coastline. The lobstermen in Portsmouth—along with many other towns—have lost thousands of dollars. Whoever is doing it is breaking the law. Stealing lobsters is a serious crime."

"Do the lobstermen think it's someone from around here?" Kate asked.

"They don't know," Luke said, "but they are holding a meeting tonight to discuss what to do."

Just then, Luke's motor sputtered briefly and then stopped completely. Luke turned around, "I wonder if the propeller got caught on a lobster-buoy line."

He pulled the motor out of the water and discovered a large, black bag wrapped around the propeller. "Is that seaweed?" Kate asked.

"No, it's a big plastic bag!" Luke said. "I can't believe the litter people just throw in the water."

As Luke worked to untangle the mess on the propeller, Kate sat watching her fishing line while the boat drifted slowly with the outgoing tide. They were heading toward the small island of Whaleback Light. She tried to stay calm but wondered if Luke would be able to get the motor running again before they drifted all the way out to sea.

A large, scaly hump quietly broke the water's surface alongside the skiff.

"LLLLLLLUKE," Kate stammered, "it's a cr... croc...crocodile!!!"

Was it a sea monster? Kate couldn't see its head or tail. The heavily scaled backbone seemed endless as it slowly moved back into the water.

"Wow!" Luke turned around just in time to see the last two feet of pointed ridges descend into the water's depth.

"I've never seen anything like it before," Luke said. "It can't be a crocodile. They don't live in saltwater, and they sure can't survive in our cold water."

"Let's get out of here," Kate said. "It might have friends!"

"I almost have the plastic off," Luke replied.

Just then a large boat approached with Ian at its helm. "Need a bit of help there, mates?" he called.

"We just saw a sea monster!" Kate shouted. "With scales on its back like a crocodile."

"Sea monster!" Ian laughed. "That's quite a fish story."

Luke glared at Ian and then finally freed the

propeller from the plastic bag.

"It was probably a sturgeon," Ian said. "They're a rare fish and have bony plates known as scutes. That's probably why it reminded Kate of a crocodile. We see them sometimes out at

Appledore, and they can get as long as fourteen feet if they're left alone. They're a protected species."

He looked down at the skiff. "Say, do you need a tow?"

Kate was about to say "yes!" when Luke got the motor started.

"No, thanks," Luke said, calmly. He wasn't about to let Ian look like the big hero who rescued them. "We're managing just fine."

As the two boats motored away from each other, Ian shouted back, "See you tomorrow morning at the dock—bright and early."

# Chapter SEVEN

The day had finally arrived, and the sun was rising over the Isles of Shoals as Uncle Rick and his group motored out to Appledore Island. The small islands were about six miles out, and on a clear day, you could see them from shore.

Luke watched Ian at the helm of the marine lab boat and was surprised his father had given Ian the honor of steering it. Ian was older, but Luke had been around boats forever and had often steered the lobster boat. Glumly, he looked at his dad, who was talking with his uncle.

Kevin Carver wore his favorite woolen cap, hiding his light-colored hair as he spoke loudly to Rick over the sound of the motor. "The lobster stealing is getting worse," Luke's father said.

"How did the meeting go last night at the fishermen's co-op?" Uncle Rick asked. "Any clues about who might be stealing the lobsters? Any ideas what's being done about it?"

"We've no idea who's doing it," said Mr. Carver, his face growing serious. "But we've decided to post guards on this week's catch until the truck from Boston picks it up to take to market."

"Hey, Dad," Luke asked, "can I steer the boat for a while?"

"Better not," his father replied. "This is a lot of boat to handle, and Ian's done it before. But you can take your skiff out around the islands once we're there."

Disappointed, Luke moved to the boat's stern where Kate and Mrs. Evans were listening to his mom talk about bringing her watercolors to paint Celia Thaxter's garden. His mother was a fan of the nineteenth-century poet and was excited to visit the island where she had lived. Luke didn't paint, but he liked taking photos. He had brought his camera and had it around his neck. He started taking pictures of his skiff as it bobbed in the waves behind the boat. As he sat, he listened to the conversation.

"Did you know Celia Thaxter offered her house as a summer retreat for artists and writers?" Kate's mom asked. "Celia also named one of her favorite spots on the island Fairy Dell."

"Kate, that means there are fairies on the island," Meg said. "We should build them some houses."

At that moment, Luke spotted a small, gray shape swimming along with the skiff.

"Look, everybody!" he shouted. "It's a seal!"

"Can you take the wheel, Mr. Carver?" Ian asked. "I think I know this seal."

Ian joined the group at the stern of the boat. "Just as I thought—it's Sookie."

"Is Sookie your pet?" Meg asked.

"No," Ian said. "Sookie is the Appledore Island mascot. She swims with the marine students when they're diving to collect samples. She's curious about everything and often follows the research boat."

"Some of the marine students found her this summer," Ian continued. "She had lost her mother, so the students fed her until she was able to feed herself. She knows the research boat and often swims out to greet it."

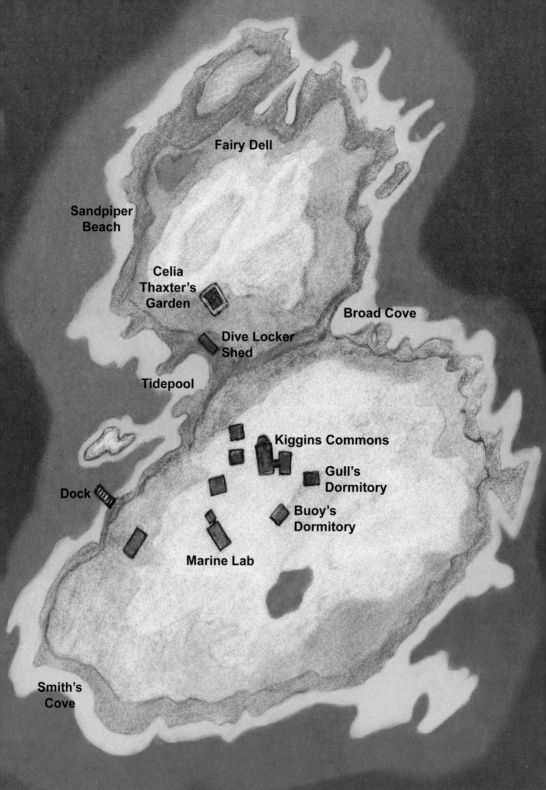

Fairy Dell

Sandpiper
Beach

Celia
Thaxter's
Garden

Dive Locker
Shed

Broad Cove

Tidepool

Dock

Kiggins Commons

Gull's
Dormitory

Buoy's
Dormitory

Marine Lab

Smith's
Cove

Sookie delighted everyone as she bobbed in and out of the waves. The entertainment made the rest of the journey to the island pass quickly.

Luke's father guided the boat up to the Appledore dock. Ian hopped out first and pointed to the few buildings on the island.

"The two largest buildings are the laboratory over there with the high tower and, to the left, my favorite one, Kiggins Commons," Ian said. "That's where the kitchen is. It has a sizable dining hall with a large deck and the best view on the island. The smaller buildings are mainly sleeping quarters, a couple more research areas and an office."

"It's smaller than I thought," Luke said as he leapt to the dock.

"We really try to run a green operation here, Luke," Ian replied. "You know, tread lightly, recycle and all that. Even the toilets here are solar-powered. Sure, we could use more buildings but that goes against our purpose here."

"What is the purpose?" Kate asked.

"Sustainability," Ian replied as he helped Luke's mom with some bags.

"Why don't you all get settled," Uncle Rick said as he finished tying up the boat. "I'm going to turn on the electricity at the wind power station."

"Where are we sleeping?" asked Luke. He was not going to ask Mr. Know-It-All what sustainability meant. He'd look it up later.

"In the dormitories behind Kiggins Commons," Ian said. "You and I are staying with your dad and uncle in the Buoys dorm. You ladies will be in the Gulls dorm."

# Chapter
# EIGHT

"Would it be possible to go swimming?" Kate asked after everyone had eaten lunch and settled into their bunk rooms.

"We brought our snorkel gear," Luke said.

"There are wetsuits in the dive locker shed at the cove," Ian said. "I'm sure there are some small enough to fit you."

"Why don't we all go down to the cove?" Mrs. Carver suggested. "Maybe I'll do some sketching."

Kate's mom agreed. "It's a treat to have such warm weather in October."

"Go ahead," Mr. Carver said. "But I'll need you, Ian, to show Rick and me where the wood shutters are kept so we can start boarding up windows."

It didn't take Kate and Luke long to find the wetsuits and put on their snorkeling gear. When they arrived at the cove, Kate's mother was looking for seashells with Meg while Mrs. Carver was busy sketching the White Island

Lighthouse in the distance.

"Wow, this water is really cold," Kate said as she waded into the tidal pool. "I thought these wetsuits were supposed to keep us warm."

"As soon as your body heats the water in your suit, you'll be warm," Luke said. "Follow me."

Kate soon found herself swimming in the tidal pool's amazingly clear water. Peering through her face mask, she saw sunlight pierce the water and illuminate the undersea world. She spied a structure of rocks adorned with shells and seaweed that looked like an underwater fairy castle.

As she swam closer, she noticed the castle was covered with starfish and prickly sea urchins, all lined up as if on guard. Until now, Kate had seen them only in man-made tanks—never in their natural environment!

She touched Luke's arm and pointed to the amazing structure. Luke gave her a big smile through his mask and a thumbs-up.

Kate felt a movement in the water behind her and turned to see a large, gray shape whoosh past them. Was it that big, scaly fish she saw from Luke's boat? She started to yell a warning to Luke and then remembered that wouldn't work underwater. She grabbed his arm just as the gray shape swam out from behind some rocks!

It was Sookie! Kate's eyes widened as the seal swam right up to her mask. They stared at each other for a long moment. Then the seal playfully circled them both and headed over to the fairy castle. She scared a lobster out of its hiding place under the seaweed before proceeding to the water's surface for some air. Kate, too, brought her head above the water and pulled out her mouthpiece. "Look Meg," she called.
"It's Sookie! She's come to say hi."

"It's the seal!" Meg laughed. "Do you think she's hungry? Can I feed her part of my apple?"

"She'll find her own food in the water,"

Kate's mom said. "Look, there she goes!"

Everybody laughed as Sookie splashed her tail at them and then headed out to deeper waters—no doubt looking for a tasty snack.

# Chapter
# NINE

That evening after dinner, Uncle Rick surprised everybody by announcing they were going to have a bonfire at the beach.

"Great," Luke said. "Can we roast marshmallows?"

"I just happen to have a bag," his mother replied with a smile.

"Grab your flashlights, everybody," Uncle Rick said, "and follow me."

Soon, they all were sitting around the crackling fire. As the moonlight cast strange shadows around them, Ian pointed to what looked like a dark patch of sand farther down the beach.

"What are you pointing at?" Luke asked. "Is there something in that shadow?"

"It's not a shadow," Ian said. "They're sandpipers."

"There must be hundreds of them," Luke's father said.

"They're migrating," Ian explained.

"They gather in large numbers to head south and are stopping over for a rest before they continue on their long journey."

Everybody sat in silence for a few moments and thought about all the miles those little birds had ahead of them.

A fog rolled in off the ocean and a beam from the lighthouse shone ghostlike through the mist. Luke jumped when the sound of a foghorn eerily broke the silence.

"Just the right atmosphere," Ian said in a mysterious whisper, "to tell the story of the Lady in White."

"Who was she?" Kate asked.

"The Lady in White was the last wife of the infamous pirate Blackbeard," Ian said. "He left her behind on these islands with his buried treasure when he escaped to avoid capture. Many people claim they have seen her ghost roaming the islands, still searching for him and calling his name."

"Is she a friendly ghost?" Meg whispered as she moved closer to her mother.

"Bedtime," Luke's father quickly announced.

"At least for you, little one." He swept Meg into his arms and jostled her into a smile.

"I think I'll join you," Luke's mom said, yawning. "I plan on getting up early to paint the sunrise."

"Kerry, would you like to take a walk?" Uncle Rick asked Mrs. Evans.

"Sure," Kate's mom replied. "Kate, I'll see you at the Gulls dorm soon."

"Don't stay out too late, Mom," Kate said, smiling to herself.

"I just have one more story to tell," Ian said to Kate and Luke.

"Is this another ghost story?" Luke asked after everyone else had gone.

"Absolutely," Ian said. "It's the story of Blackbeard's pet walrus. He acquired it when he and his band of pirates robbed a British ship that was headed back from the north. The great beast was in the hull, destined to become a new attraction at some zoo. Blackbeard trained the walrus to obey him and terrorize his enemies. Rumor has it that the ghost of the walrus haunts these waters, protecting the pirate's hidden treasure."

"Oh, right," Luke said. "Talk about fish stories. Come on, Kate, let's head back. I'm sure Ian can manage to put the fire out himself."

"You may mock," Ian called as they walked up the hill. "But beware the Wrath of the Wicked Walrus!"

"Do you believe that guy?" Luke asked Kate as they neared the dorms. "He sure likes to be the center of attention."

"I think he's kind of fun," Kate said. "I like his stories. You're not jealous of him, are you, Luke?"

"No way!" Luke proclaimed loudly.

"Are you sure?" Kate called as they headed to their separate dorms.

# Chapter
# TEN

"I'm not jealous—not one bit," Luke mumbled to himself as he brushed his teeth at the sink. "That was the dumbest story I ever heard. What does he think I am ... a two-year-old?!"

As he approached the dorm room, he heard snoring, a sure sign his father was already fast asleep. Luke picked up one of the flashlights by the door and tiptoed into the room. It sure is dark on this island, he thought as he headed toward his bunk bed. Not only weren't there any streetlights, but fog had completely covered the moon. The foghorn sounded sinister as it called its mournful warning to ships at sea.

Luke had just settled himself in the top bunk when he heard a scraping noise at the window. He swung his flashlight beam at the glass. There was a huge, bony face with two enormous protruding tusks staring right at him. Even through the glare of the reflected light on

the glass, Luke knew he was looking at THE WALRUS!

His heart pounded and goose bumps popped up on his arms. Then the giant face disappeared.

"Was that real? Was it the fog? Did I imagine it?" Luke had to find out. Taking some deep breaths, he picked up his flashlight and headed into the night.

Slowly, Luke walked around the building, checking every window. "I wonder where Ian is," he thought suspiciously. Luke headed down to the beach where the campfire had been. It was smothered in seaweed, and no one—people or walruses—was around.

Luke sat down to think. Had he actually seen the walrus skull? Perhaps it was just the fog. Maybe being on an island way out at sea could play tricks on your mind. The stars started to appear in the night sky again, and the moon peeked out from behind the moving clouds. Its light spilled so brightly across the ocean to the other islands that Luke could make out the doors and windows at the large, white hotel on Star Island just a short distance away.

Then Luke noticed another light bobbing up and down on one side of the old hotel. "A flashlight?" he wondered. "Isn't the hotel closed for the winter? Who would be there?" He looked back, and the light had disappeared. "Was that my imagination, too? Maybe I just need some sleep. I probably should get back to the dorm before Uncle Rick does."

Luke hurried back to his bunk, wondering if he should tell Kate about any of this. Would she make fun of him? Or worse, would she tell Ian?

# Chapter ELEVEN

"What's for breakfast?" Kate yawned as she entered the dining room at Kiggins Commons.

"Blueberry pancakes!" Luke's dad announced. "Connie is out painting already, so Rick and I are the cooks this morning."

Kate watched her mother give Rick a big smile as he poured maple syrup on the pancakes. Her mother had been alone since Kate's father died when she was a baby. Kate liked Luke's uncle, and it was obvious that her mother did, too.

After breakfast, Mr. Carver told Ian and Luke to grab some wooden shutters from under the deck, and then join him and Rick up by the lab building.

As Kate was putting away the dishes, she could see Luke trying to keep up with Ian's long stride as they carried a couple of shutters between them. "I hope they can become friends," she thought. "They are more alike than they know."

Her thoughts were interrupted when her mom said, "Come on, Kate and Meg, our job this morning is to put Celia Thaxter's garden to bed for the winter."

On the way to the garden, they stopped at a shed to pick up a rake. Kate noticed a worn map of Appledore Island tacked to the wall. On the north end was an area marked Fairy Dell.

"Mom, did Celia Thaxter believe in fairies?" Kate asked.

"It's possible," her mom replied. "Fairies were very popular in England at that time."

"Could I borrow that map this afternoon?" Kate asked.

"Of course," her mom said. "I know how you and Luke like to explore. Just remember to return it."

When they got to the garden, Mrs. Carver was finishing up at her easel. "It reminds me of Mrs. Lennox's garden, only smaller," Kate said as she looked at the painting. "It's really colorful."

"I'm starting to paint like the Impressionist artists who stayed in Celia Thaxter's home,"

Mrs. Carver laughed as she pushed back a loose strand of her long, wavy hair.

Kate noticed that Mrs. Carver had big, brown eyes with thick lashes—the same as her brother and children. They all had beautiful skin that always looked tanned. Kate, on the other hand, was pale like her mom and seemed only to get more freckles from the sun.

Kate looked past the garden to a stone foundation that defined where Celia's home once stood. "What happened to Celia's house?" Kate asked her mom.

"It was destroyed in a fire in 1914 along with a big hotel her father had built," Mrs. Evans replied. "People from that time would come here from all over New England for their summer vacations. We can research more about it in the library when we get back."

"Mrs. Lennox says her house will probably be burned to the ground and there will just be grass, like here" Kate said. "She thinks it's better than letting someone build hundreds of condos all over her land."

A small head popped up over the dried stalks in the flower beds. "Hey, Kate," Meg called. "I found a hop-toad. Do you think it swam all the way here from our house?"

Mrs. Carver laughed. "Celia probably brought toads out to the islands when she lived here."

"That would make sense," Kate said. "Toads protect gardens by eating the slugs and insects that like to eat the plants."

"Let's make the toad a fairy house," Meg said.

"Sure," Kate replied. "We can use these dry flower stalks and fallen leaves."

They set to work building what Kate called a "toad abode," while Kate's mom raked and Mrs. Carver painted. "Now the hop-toad will have a place to stay warm this winter," Meg said.

# Chapter TWELVE

As they headed to the lab, Luke kept glancing at Ian's face, looking for any signs of mischief. Luke still couldn't believe he had imagined that giant walrus ghost—or whatever it was. He was too old to believe there was a spirit of any kind lurking around the island ... wasn't he?

When they reached the lab building, Luke found his dad and Uncle Rick busy on a ladder outside the building, securing shutters over one of the windows.

"Grab a broom, Luke," his father called. "You both can start cleaning inside."

The door creaked as Ian shoved it open, and Luke followed him into the dark lab. Ian switched on a light and Luke gasped. There in front of him were long shelves of jars filled with pickled sea animals and plants. Along the far wall hung a couple of shark jawbones still holding most of their teeth. Next to that was the biggest lobster shell Luke had ever seen.

"You don't find many that big anymore," said his father, nodding at the lobster as he handed Luke a dustpan.

"Dad, do you think they'll catch the thief who is stealing the lobsters?" Luke asked.

"I hope so, Luke," his father replied. "They think there has to be more than one person doing the stealing. If they're smart, they'll stop because now the Coast Guard is looking for them, too. The more people who keep watch, the better the chances that the thieves will be caught."

"Hey, mate," Ian said. "I could use some help here."

"Right," Luke said. He went to the far side of the large room where the windows had already been boarded up. It took him a minute to notice the enormous skeleton stretched above him that hung from the rafters. Luke thought it must be a whale, but he certainly wasn't going to ask Ian.

"Soooo...," Ian asked casually as he handed Luke a broom. "How did you sleep last night, Luke?"

"Great," Luke said. "Why are you asking?"

"I mean I hope those noisy seagulls didn't keep you awake," Ian said. "It drives the summer kids crazy the way those birds squawk and make crash landings on the metal roof right at the crack of dawn."

"Didn't even hear them," Luke replied, which was true. After his late-night adventure, he had slept very soundly.

"Glad to hear it," Ian said. Luke stole a look at Ian and was sure a sneaky smile appeared briefly on the older boy's face.

"You know," Ian said, "there is a great little cove on the west side of the island called Sandpiper Beach. I could take you and the girls over there, and we can go exploring. I've always thought if I had been a pirate, that's where I would bury my treasure."

"Why not?" Luke said coolly, imagining Ian with a patch over his eye and a pirate's hat on his head. And maybe a parrot on his shoulder ...

"Great," Ian interrupted Luke's thoughts. "We'll head out after lunch."

Exploring was something Luke was always up for—even with Ian ... the pirate!

# Chapter THIRTEEN

After lunch, Luke packed two knapsacks with banana bread, apples and water for the expedition. Ian stuffed towels into his pack, and picked up Meg's small pail and shovel. "I know this great area for finding shells," he told her. "And we should look for sea glass. I bring sea glass and old china shards home to my sister who makes jewelry from them."

"Wow, I wish I had a brother like you," Kate said.

Ian added, "And Luke wants to dig for pirate's treasure. Right, Luke?"

"Let's just get going," Luke said, ignoring the question.

At the bottom of the porch steps, there was a pile of sticks roughly three-feet long. Ian handed a stick to each of the explorers. "When I tell you, hold these up above your heads as we walk," he said.

"Why would we do that?" Luke asked.

"Oh, you'll find out soon enough," Ian said.

"Well, I don't need one," said Luke, thinking Ian was planning another joke.

"Suit yourself," Ian said with a grin.

They followed a worn path heading to the shoreline that led past clumps of tea-rose thickets. As the kids approached the cove, they could see seagulls everywhere. Ian shouted, "Sticks up, everybody!"

Luke watched Kate and Meg raise their sticks above their heads. Suddenly a huge seagull with black wings took flight from the rocky cliffs. It dove straight down at the only person who was not holding a stick. Luke started running but wasn't fast enough. He yelped when the large claws grazed his thick hair, just missing his scalp! He tried to wave his hands to scare off the huge seagull, but the bird dove at him again. White seagull droppings hit Luke's head and splattered down his back.

"Killer has honored you!" Ian was beside himself with laughter. "Don't say I didn't try to warn you, Luke."

Kate and Meg laughed, too, as the slimy white goop dripped down Luke's face.

"You should have brought your camera, Luke," Ian said, grinning. "What I wouldn't give for a picture of you right now!"

Without replying, Luke marched down to the water's edge and kept walking until he was waist high in the ocean. Then he bent his knees and plunged his head in the water.

"Master Killer is a black-winged seagull and the largest of his species," Ian laughed. "He thinks he owns this island and is known for his unique form of defense. Killer and his missus nest here every year. When unsuspecting victims come too near their home, he attacks— even when there aren't any eggs or fledglings in the nest to protect."

"You still have a little white goop on the back of your head," Kate said with sympathy as she handed Luke a towel.

Meg took Ian's hand. "Would you build a beach fairy house with me?" she asked.

"What a grand idea!" Ian said, playing along.

"Let's make it big enough for you to play in, Meg. You can be our fairy princess."

"Let's build it right here," Kate said, "under this ridge of rocks above the tide line."

Everyone joined in the building. Ian collected driftwood branches and placed them against the rocks like a lean-to. Kate found seaweed and draped it over the branches like a roof. Luke rolled over a couple of large rocks to help hold the sticks in place. Meg collected seagull feathers for decoration.

"How about using this?" Ian held up a colorful lobster buoy.

"Fairies don't like anything artificial," Kate said. "They like things from nature." She draped more seaweed to hang down like a curtain over the house's doorway.

"Kate, do you want to come into my house for tea?" Meg asked. The two of them just fit inside. Kate mimicked pouring tea into two large clamshells Meg found.

While Meg and Kate played in the fairy house, Ian searched for sea glass. Luke spent his time exploring the tidal pools, turning up rocks to see how many crabs he could find.

The afternoon passed quickly, and Ian offered a tired Meg a piggyback ride on the way back to the main building.

"Playing the hero again," Luke thought, as he carried Ian's pack along with his own.

# Chapter FOURTEEN

That night, the moon was full and Ian brought the lab's telescope onto the deck after dinner. "I can't believe how detailed the moon's craters are through the telescope," Kate said as they all took turns looking.

"October is the month of the Harvest Moon," Uncle Rick said.

"Harvest Moon was the time when the Native Americans knew their corn, pumpkins and wild rice were ready for harvest," Kate's mom explained. "The food was stored to help feed them through the winter."

"Look at those tiny, bright highlights on the moon's surface," Luke's mom said.

"Are those fairies on the moon?" Meg asked when it was her turn.

"Let me see," Luke said. Staring through the telescope, he thought the shadows of the moon's craters looked a lot like the face of a walrus. "No," he thought, backing away from the eyepiece just in time to see a shooting star streak across the sky. "Did you see that?" he asked.

"I missed it," Uncle Rick replied. "But look," he pointed, "do you see the moving star? That's a satellite."

"We'll probably see more if we stay out here longer," Ian said. "There are hundreds of them in space sending information throughout the world."

Everyone in the group looked up for a while, watching for satellites and enjoying the peaceful night. The moon and stars, and the sound of the ocean, seemed to fill the night with enchantment.

Soon, it was Meg's bedtime and her parents took her inside for a bedtime story. "I've got some reading to do myself," Ian said. "Good night, everyone."

"I'm up for a walk in the moonlight," Rick said. "Anybody else want to join me?"

"Can we come, too?" Kate asked, without waiting for her mom or Luke to reply.

The four decided to walk to Broad Cove. Instead of a sandy beach, this cove was filled with rocks of all sizes. Luke picked up a flat stone and sent it skipping across the water.

Wherever the stone struck the water, a sparkling, green light bloomed.

"Wow, that's beautiful," Kate said, as Luke sent a second stone bouncing, creating another shimmering, green path in its wake.

"That's phosphorescence," Uncle Rick explained. "It's the same stuff that's in lightning bugs, only these are small marine animals. I think the movement in the water causes them to light up."

"My grandmother used to tell me," Kate's mom said, "that when the ocean sparkled at night, the mermaids were dancing underwater."

They all sat for a while, enjoying the evening's magic filled with moonlight and sea sparkles. Soon, Uncle Rick and Kate's mom decided to take a short, moonlight stroll to the garden, while Luke and Kate headed for the dorms.

After Luke said goodnight to Kate, he noticed a light on in the lab building. He crept quietly to a crack in the boarded window and peered in. The light suddenly switched off, but not before he saw a huge, wooden box that wasn't there before. Next to it was a walrus skull!

Luke jumped when a hand landed on his shoulder.

"Luke, my man," Ian chuckled, "you act as if you've seen a ghost."

Before Luke could answer, Ian pointed over his shoulder. "Hey, do you see that light coming from the old hotel on Star Island?"

Luke looked across the channel to the neighboring island and saw a light flickering. This time it was coming from inside the great hotel. He hadn't imagined it after all!

"How could someone be over there?" Ian asked thoughtfully. "It's closed up for the season. What do you say we take the skiff over there tomorrow? We could check it out and explore the island."

"Sure," Luke said as they headed to the Buoys dorm. He decided not to tell Ian that he knew the truth about the walrus prank.

 **Chapter FIFTEEN**

At sunrise, everyone gathered in the cafeteria for an early breakfast.

"No sleeping in this morning," Mrs. Carver said. "What was all that racket on the roof so early?"

"Just the seagulls fighting over food," Ian replied as he poured milk on a large bowl of cereal.

"When they land on this metal roof," Mr. Carver said, "it's like the crash of cymbals in an orchestra."

"Dad," Luke said, "Ian and I saw something strange over on Star Island last night ..." But before Luke could finish, his dad's marine radio crackled and sputtered to life on a nearby table.

Mr. Carver's face turned serious as he carried the radio into the next room.

"I wonder what's up at the fishing co-op," Uncle Rick said.

In a few minutes, Mr. Carver came back to the cafeteria, looking very upset.

"It's bad news," he said. "Someone stole the whole week's lobster catch from the holding area last night. The fisherman on guard was tied up and gagged. They even stole one of our fishing boats to drag the cages away. The lobsters and boat are probably worth half a million dollars."

"What are you going to do, Kevin?" Uncle Rick asked.

"I need to head back right away," Luke's dad replied. "You can stay here with Ian and Luke, and finish up."

"Meg and I will come back with you," Mrs. Carver said.

"The weather's so beautiful," Mrs. Evans said. "I think Kate and I will stay and help out here."

Twenty minutes later, they all headed down to the dock. As they were loading the boat, Kate saw Sookie lying still on the sand over by the tidal pool.

"Look!" Kate cried. "There's Sookie, and I think something's wrong with her."

Luke's mom grabbed the first aid kit from the boat, and they all hurried over to the small beach to get a closer look at the young seal. When Sookie weakly lifted her head, they saw a large gash near her right fin. Ian and Mrs. Carver got to work and managed to stop the bleeding by wrapping bandages around the wound.

Ian looked in the boat shed and found a tarp; together, they managed to slip it under the young seal. With Luke and Ian joining

Mr. Carver and Uncle Rick, they each lifted a
corner of the makeshift stretcher. Sookie lay still,
but her large eyes were open and alert.

"Let's get her on the boat," Mr. Carver said.
"There's a special rescue group on the mainland
that can help her. Rick, take this extra radio
in case you need to contact us. I'll be back
tomorrow afternoon to pick everyone up."

Soon the boat was headed out, leaving Luke's skiff behind. As they all waved goodbye, Kate could see Meg comforting Sookie.

Uncle Rick turned to Luke. "It's strange. That cut on the seal looked like a knife wound. It's illegal to hunt seals in these waters, and it's got me wondering. Luke, what were you saying earlier about seeing something on Star Island?"

Before Luke could answer, Ian interrupted him. "Last night, we saw a light moving around in the hotel."

"That is strange," Uncle Rick said. "Ian, let's take the skiff and row over there to check it out."

"Can I go?" Luke asked. He couldn't believe Uncle Rick would rather take Ian instead of him.

"I'd feel better not leaving Kerry and Kate alone," Rick replied. "I'd like you to stay here. It shouldn't take us long."

"We'll be back before you know it, mate!" Ian said.

# Chapter SIXTEEN

"They should be back from Star Island by now," Luke complained as Kate's mom heated up some chowder for dinner. "It's been more than five hours."

"We'll eat our dinner now," Kate's mom said, "and I'll save some for them when they get back."

After the meal, Kate said, "Why don't we go back to Broad Cove? It faces east, and we can watch the moon rise."

"Take your flashlights; it's starting to get dark," her mom said. "I'll stay here and wait for the workers."

"I keep wondering how Sookie got hurt," Kate said as they walked along the path past the boarded-up marine lab.

"Something or someone must have attacked her," Luke replied. "But it didn't look like bite marks. It was more of a slash, and Uncle Rick thinks it was made by a knife."

As the ocean came into view, Kate and Luke could see the full moon just peeking over the ocean, like a giant orange. It sent a golden path of light across the water, all the way to Broad Cove.

"Do you think your uncle and Ian are all right?" Kate asked. "It's getting dark now and won't be easy to see. I overheard Ian tell Rick that you both saw a light coming from the hotel the other night."

"I'm not sure what I saw," Luke replied. "But Star Island is pretty close. Besides, the full moon is lighting the water better than any streetlights could."

"You're probably right," Kate said. "I bet they're back at the kitchen eating Mom's chowder right now."

"Look, Kate," Luke said as he pointed to a

pair of fins breaking the water's surface close
to the shore.

"Are those sharks?" Kate asked.

"No, they're porpoises," Luke replied.

"You mean like Flipper?" Kate asked.

"No, Flipper was a dolphin," Luke answered.
"The two species are closely related, but
porpoises are smaller and have a shorter snout.
Porpoises can live in colder waters and are very
shy. Listen, Kate, we're so close you can hear
them blowing air from their blowholes!"

Kate and Luke stood very quietly, listening
to the pffffooofff sound as each porpoise rose to
blow out water and take in air before descending
back in the moonlit ocean.

"Do you think there are any whales out there,
Luke?" Kate wondered.

"There could be some migrating a little farther out," Luke said.

"It's pretty dark," said Kate, turning on her flashlight. "We should head back."

As they rounded the corner past the dive locker shed, they stopped suddenly. Strange voices drifted down from the deck of the Kiggins Commons.

"Shh," Luke said. "Who's that with your mom? It's not Uncle Rick."

Kate and Luke turned off their flashlights and crept closer. The rough voice became clearer.

"I want to know if there is anyone else here on the island besides you and your boyfriend," said a large man with a beard. "He should have kept his nose away from our business instead of interfering where he wasn't wanted."

"Rick and I are the only ones on the island," Kate's mom said. "Where is he? What have you done with him!?"

"Locked him up on the boat where he won't give us any more trouble," growled a second man. "And you'd better be telling the truth about no one else being here!"

"Lock her in the bathroom where she can't cause any mischief," the bearded man said. "We'll decide what to do with her later."

"What are we going to do?" Kate gasped. "They've got Mom!"

"They've got Uncle Rick, too," Luke whispered. "But where's Ian?"

"Don't get any ideas, lady," the bearded man said as he pushed Kate's mom inside. "We have the radio. Just do what we say, and you won't get hurt."

"Luke," Kate said, "we have to rescue her!"

"We need to get help," Luke replied. "There might be an extra radio over at the lab. Let's sneak over there."

Quietly, they crept around Kiggins Commons and slowly made their way to the marine lab. They tiptoed up the porch steps, and Luke cautiously opened the door. Kate gasped. An enormous walrus loomed in front of them!

Luke switched on his flashlight just as Ian stepped out from behind the giant figure. "Luke! Kate! You're all right!" he said. "I thought those two thugs had captured you, too!"

# Chapter SEVENTEEN

"Where's Uncle Rick?" Luke whispered as he and Kate watched Ian wrap a white, canvas sheet around the ladder that held up the walrus skull.

"They knocked him out and tied him up in the cabin of the big fishing boat that's down at the dock," Ian said.

"What happened on Star Island?" Kate asked.

"When we got there," Ian said, "it looked like someone had broken into the main hotel. Rick went in to investigate and sent me to check the smaller buildings. One of those men must have been hiding in the hotel and caught Rick by surprise."

"How did you get away?" Luke asked.

"Just before I got to the Stone Chapel," Ian said, "I spooked a great horned owl. He was huge, and I just stood there, stunned, for a minute as he glided over me and headed toward a cove on the south side. Owls are rare out here, so I decided to follow him. That's when I heard an engine start and saw a large boat in the cove below me. As it started to motor away, I could see a floating island of lobster cages tied near the shore hidden from view."

"The stolen boat from the fishing co-op!" Luke gasped.

"They must be the lobster thieves," Kate said.

"I ran back to tell Rick," Ian continued. "But when I got to the hotel, it was too late. I could see that your uncle was unconscious and the guy had tied him up. He was pushing your uncle in a wheelbarrow out to the dock. I ducked behind the hotel before that guy could see me. In minutes, the boat I discovered came around the bend and pulled in. It didn't take long for those two thugs to get Rick onboard and head to Appledore Island."

"What about Rick's radio?" Kate asked. "We need to call for help!"

"And where's my skiff?" Luke asked.

"Those two goons smashed the radio," Ian said. "And they cut your skiff loose and let her drift. But luckily, nature was on my side. The tide was going out, and your boat was grounded on a sandbar. I waded out, jumped in

and rowed back to Appledore so they wouldn't
hear the boat's motor. I landed at Smith's Cove
where they wouldn't see me."

Ian stopped talking as he inspected the
walrus booby trap. "This should do it," he
said. "Luke, you and Kate need to get to the
stolen boat and grab the marine radio. Run to
somewhere safe and call the Coast Guard
for help."

"Aren't you coming with us?" Kate asked.

"I'm going to cause a diversion here with
Wally the Walrus. A little trick I used to do on

unsuspecting students." Ian paused as he looked at Luke. "And others."

Luke opened the door. "The coast is clear," he whispered.

"I'll give you a ten-minute head start," Ian said. "Go, and good luck!"

# Chapter EIGHTEEN

"Darn, it's locked!" Luke said, pulling on the cabin door of the boat.

"Do you think your uncle's in there?" Kate whispered.

"If he is, he's still unconscious," Luke said. "I hope he's okay. We have to find that radio and get some help here fast."

"Look, Luke!" cried Kate, pointing up the hill to a flashing light in the lab's doorway. "Ian must be starting his diversion."

"She lied!" Kate and Luke could hear the loud voice of the bearded man from the deck of the dining hall. "There IS someone else on this island. I'm going over there to see who it is. You go make sure the boyfriend is still tied up on the boat."

"Kate!" Luke said in a loud whisper. "We've got to get out of here!"

As they headed away from the dock, a flashlight beam shone a short distance behind them. "Hey! Where'd you kids come from?"

The second thief shouted, "Get back here!"

"Run, Luke!" Kate exclaimed. "Follow me!"

"Where are we going?" Luke panted as he followed Kate toward Sandpiper Beach.

"We can hide in the fairy house!" Kate said.

When they approached the cove, Luke whispered, "We need to move quietly. Remember, this is Killer's territory."

"There's the house," Kate said, pointing. "It's under those rocks."

They quickly squeezed into the cramped space, and Kate pulled some of the seaweed roof down over the opening. Then they waited, straining their ears and barely breathing. Soon they heard their pursuer stumbling in the darkness.

"He's going to wake up Killer with all that noise," Luke whispered.

Just then, they heard a loud screeching and the flapping of great wings.

"Owww! Get away, you lousy bird!" the thief cried out.

"It sounds like Killer is dive-bombing," Luke said, "and that thug doesn't have a stick!"

"Cut it out, you crazy seagull!" They heard the thief curse.

The light from the man's flashlight bobbed just above the fairy house. Kate shut her eyes. Would he discover their hiding place?

A bloodcurdling scream sent shivers down her spine. There was an enormous crash, and several stones and a flashlight tumbled down in front of their hideaway. The light beam bounced over the seaweed until it settled at the opening of the fairy house.

Then everything went quiet. It was as though the thief and the seagull had vanished in the night. After waiting a little longer, Luke slowly lifted the seaweed curtain and peered out. "I think Killer has conquered our enemy for us," Luke said as he picked up the fallen flashlight.

Crawling out of the fairy house, Kate and Luke could see an arm dangling over the rocks above them. When the arm remained motionless, the children slowly approached the large body lying face down on the rocks. Luke shone the flashlight on a large gash at the top of the thief's head.

"Is he dead?" Kate whispered.

"I don't think so," Luke replied. "But we've got to get away in case he recovers. We have to go back to save your mom and Uncle Rick."

Luke held Kate's arm, and they carefully crept around the man, while staying low enough to avoid attracting Killer's attention.

Luke's heart leapt into his throat as a crackling voice sputtered from beneath the man's body.

"Pirates on the Isles, Pirates on the Isles, come in please!"

"Run, Luke!" Kate shouted. "He's ALIVE!!!"

"No, wait," Luke said. "Kate, it's the marine radio. It's underneath him. I can see the antenna sticking out."

"This is Redbeard confirming meeting time of twenty-four hundred hours," said the crusty voice coming from the belly of the thief.

"I need to get that radio," Luke said.

"Here, use this." Kate handed Luke a long stick. He placed the end of the stick under the thief's stomach.

"He's as heavy as a whale," Luke said, as he

pushed up on the stick and tried to roll the body over. He managed to move the man just enough to expose half the radio.

"You'll have to grab it, Kate," Luke said. "Hurry, I can't hold this much longer."

Kate held her breath, grabbed the end of the radio with both hands and yanked. She fell on her backside but had the prize in her hands. She handed it to Luke who switched it off.

"Come on," Luke said. "We need to get away in case he wakes up."

# Chapter NINETEEN

As Kate and Luke were creeping cautiously along the path toward the boat, the voices of Ian and Kate's mom carried across the water. "Thanks for rescuing me, Ian. But where are Kate and Luke?"

"They were supposed to be here," Ian said as he pried open the boat's cabin door with a crowbar.

Suddenly, a series of loud crashing blows came from the lab building. A small, black cloud rose from the porch into the moonlight and separated in a flurry of small winged bats.

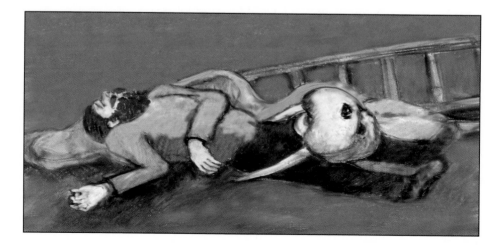

Then a huge white skull with tusks flew through the broken shutters and tumbled down the porch steps. A beam of light shone through the broken window.

"Darn it!" Ian said. "He must have woken up! I bolted the door after the walrus skull knocked him out, but now he's used the walrus's tusks to hammer his way through!"

A leg appeared from the shattered window as a flashlight beam bobbed up and down. The man struggled to fit through, but his size made it difficult.

Suddenly, two gunshots shattered the night's stillness.

"He has a gun!" Ian said. "Don't worry, Mrs. Evans. I have an idea. He doesn't know about Kate and Luke being on the island. Lock yourself in the cabin with Rick, and stay down. The hull of the boat is solid steel so you'll be safe if you stay below. I'll push the boat out to sea and it will act as a decoy. That guy will be more interested in saving the boat, it's his only way off the island. Once you free Rick, he can head the boat back to Portsmouth for help."

"Hurry, Ian!" Mrs. Evans said. "You know this island. Find Kate and Luke, and hide. I'll tend to Rick."

Ian grabbed an orange bag of emergency flares and jumped to the dock. He untied the boat and shoved it away from the pier before taking off down the path away from the main buildings.

# Chapter TWENTY

"We've got to stay hidden, Kate," Luke said.

"Shhh," Kate whispered. "Someone's coming!"

A figure ran past Luke. "Ian!" Luke said a bit too loudly as he recognized the older boy in the moonlight.

"Luke?" Ian asked. "Is Kate with you? Where's the other thief?"

"I'm here," Kate said as she and Luke stood up. "And I think the other guy is dead!"

"Knocked out, more likely," Luke said. "He got in a battle with Killer and lost."

"You found a radio!" Ian said, seeing it in Luke's hand.

"Yes," Luke replied. "I've sent a mayday to the Coast Guard in Portsmouth, and they're on their way. They should be here soon."

"We've got to go help my mom!" Kate said.

"And Uncle Rick," Luke said. "That guy has a gun!"

"Don't worry, your uncle and Kate's mother

are hiding in the cabin of the fishing boat," Ian said. "I cut the boat loose from the dock, so they should be safe."

They all looked toward the boat, which had drifted a short distance away from the shore.

"Oh, no!" Kate cried. A bulky form had jumped off the dock and was swimming toward the boat. "He's still trying to get on the boat!"

"Come on," Ian said as the three of them raced toward the tidal pool. Stopping behind a shed near the cove, Ian took the flare kit from his jacket.

Kate saw three tubes that looked like firecrackers.

"Is that a gun?" she asked.

"Sort of," Ian answered as he shoved the flare stick into the orange cylinder. "It's a flare launcher." He stood up and aimed the flare at the figure in the water.

An orange jet whooshed out in a brilliant, arching stream and landed in the water near the thief.

"Nice shot," Luke said as Ian loaded a second flare.

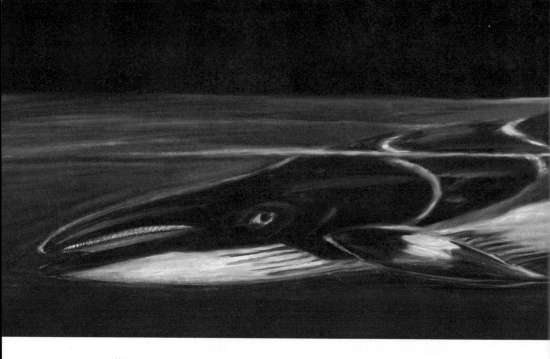

"Your turn, mate," Ian said. "Shoot it straight up, just in case the Coast Guard has any doubts about where we are."

Luke shot, and the flare took off like a red comet trying to reach the moon.

"I can't believe this!" Ian cried. "He's almost made it to the boat!"

They all ran to the dock.

"Where's the Coast Guard?" Kate cried. "Why aren't they here yet?"

"Look!" Ian said. "Do you see what I see?" They all stared toward the boat, watching as the thief mysteriously started rising up from

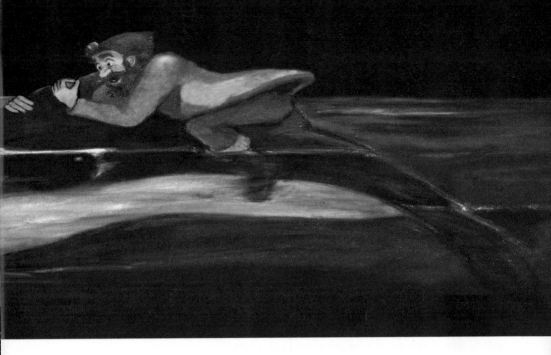

the water. Shouting in surprise, the large man struggled to hang on to a huge shape beneath him.

Kate's mouth dropped open. "Is that a rock moving?" she asked.

"Could it be a submarine?" Luke asked, as the broad, oval shape kept rising out of the water and moving swiftly away from the boat.

"It's a whale!" Ian shouted.

Amazed, they all watched the comic scene of the thief riding piggyback and hanging on for his life as the gentle giant beneath bobbed them both out to sea.

"Yep," Ian said, breaking the silence first. "It's a minke whale. Rare to see one this near shore, but they are known to be very curious critters and that flare might have brought her closer to investigate."

They all jumped as a horn bellowed out a piercing warning. Lights rippled across the dark water and a Coast Guard boat came into view.

"Just in time," Ian smiled as he handed Kate the flare launcher. "Would you like to do the honors and shoot the last flare?"

## Chapter
## TWENTY ONE

Five days later, Luke raced to Annie Lennox's house with the Portsmouth newspaper tucked under his arm. He wanted to give Ian a copy before he returned to England.

In the newspaper was a feature article about how the lobster-theft mystery had been solved. The paper reported that the two crooks had stolen a boat and dragged the floating lobster cages from the fishermen's pier out to a hidden cove behind Star Island.

At midnight the next evening, the thieves were supposed to meet a larger ship that would take the lobsters out of the country. But the plan had been foiled by Kate, Ian and Luke, who, the story said, had heroically saved the day!

Mrs. Lennox was holding a party for the three heroes in her music room, and Ian's dad had flown in from England especially for the occasion. As Luke passed all the cars parked at Creek Farm, he saw Kate in the open doorway waving to him. She was wearing a sky-blue skirt and a vest that was covered in small, sparkling dragonflies. He had rarely seen Kate when she wasn't dressed for the outdoors.

"You look really nice tonight, Kate," Luke said as he paused at the entrance.

"Thanks, Luke," Kate said with a smile. "We need to hurry, everyone is waiting!"

Hesitating at the door, Luke looked into a room filled with people. He recognized several neighbors surrounding Mrs. Lennox and his parents. There were lobstermen who worked with his dad, school friends and even Coast Guard representatives in their official uniforms.

"Hey, here he is," said Ian's familiar voice as he came into view. "This is Luke Carver, Dad, the amazing fellow I was telling you about."

Luke's mouth dropped open at Ian's words of praise. Ian's father smiled as he reached out to shake Luke's hand.

"Yep, Luke and Kate managed to bring down one of those crooks all by themselves," Ian said as he winked at Luke. "They even figured out how to get a local seagull we know to lend them a helping hand."

"Can I have your attention, please?" One of the Coast Guard officials quieted everyone down with a loud bellow. "My name is Patrick Chase, and I have the pleasure to be here today to award a medal of honor to three people whose remarkable actions helped save an important industry in our community. These friends are responsible for the capture of the culprits behind the lobster thefts, and our town has gathered here today in thanks. Would Luke Carver, Kate Evans and Ian Darby please come to the front of the room?"

Luke, Kate and Ian headed up together as people applauded. Luke felt like an Olympic winner as a medal was placed around his neck. He looked out, over the crowd, and saw his mom with tears in her eyes. He smiled when he saw his Uncle Rick next to Kate's mom. Rick smiled back and, even though his arm was in a cast, managed to give Luke a thumbs-up.

"Before you finish," Annie Lennox spoke up, "I have an announcement, too." Everyone looked expectantly at Mrs. Lennox.

"Having everyone gathered here makes it a perfect time to tell you what I have decided to do with Creek Farm," she said. "As you know, the thirty acres of land are going to the New Hampshire Department of Forestry. However, they do not want my house because of its needed repairs and maintenance. Until yesterday, I thought my home would be taken down and cleared away."

At this, there were murmurs through the crowd, but Mrs. Lennox continued. "Today, we have another hero here," she said. "Mr. Darby has informed me that Cornell University wants to use the house as a learning center for the school's marine research program. Professors will hold classes and conferences in the large rooms downstairs, and the many bedrooms will provide sleeping quarters for visiting students and teachers."

Mr. Darby continued the story. "A dock will be built on Sagamore Creek," he said, "and we will be able to transport students and faculty from here to Appledore Island. To keep the island environment sustainable, we have always been limited in what we can build out there. When my son Ian told me about this wonderful house, I knew it was just what the university needed to help expand its marine programs."

Mrs. Lennox smiled. "It just tickles my heart to know the home will be cared for and enjoyed by people who love the sea and all the creatures that call it home," she said proudly.

Applause and cheers filled the music room. Kate, Luke and Ian were soon surrounded by people asking questions about their adventure. The lady from the paper cornered Mrs. Lennox and Ian's dad to get more information about the university's plans for the old mansion.

"Luke, I'm thirsty," Kate said. "Let's grab something to eat before all the brownies are gone."

As they passed the doorway, Luke noticed a movement by the window and spied a chipmunk entering the room through a hole in the screen. He tapped Kate's shoulder, and pointed as the chipmunk found some peanuts on the floor and

stuffed his cheeks full. Luke and Kate watched the animal escape through the door and scurry to edge of the yard. They laughed when he disappeared into the discarded pumpkin that had been Kate's Halloween fairy house.

# Chapter
# TWENTY TWO

"It's nice to get out on a January weekend," Mrs. Lennox said. "I haven't been to the New England Aquarium in years, and it feels like summer in here. Look at this gigantic fish tank! It's higher than my house!"

"Thank you for bringing us here, Mrs. Lennox," said Kate, taking off her coat. "This is one of my favorite places."

"Kate, I thought we agreed you all would call me Annie," Mrs. Lennox said. "It makes me feel like one of the gang somehow."

"Thanks, Annie," Luke said. "The train ride to Boston was great!"

"Come on, Annie," Meg said. "We need to see the penguins."

"Penguins?" Annie asked. "They have penguins living in Boston? Aren't they from the South Pole?"

"They're rockhoppers," Kate said, reading the sign. "It says here that rockhoppers live on the shores of the Antarctic islands. The species got

112

its name because these penguins hop over rocks and crevices."

"I bet Ian knows all about them," Luke said.

"It's good they can hop," Annie said, "because those small, skinny wings weren't made to fly."

"But look what great swimmers they are," Kate said. Everyone watched a penguin jet through the water and propel himself onto the stone ledge—all while carrying something in his beak.

"He's got a pebble," Luke said, as the penguin waddled over to a pile of stones nestled against the rocks and carefully added the new one. "He seems to be building something with them."

"Look! He's building a fairy house," Meg said.

"You know, it does look like the foundation for a house," Annie said. "I suppose fairy houses would be built of stones in Antarctica where there wouldn't be trees."

"Looks like you're my group," a friendly voice said.

The four visitors turned to see a woman
dressed in a uniform.

"Hi," she said. "My name is Jen, and I'll be
your guide to see the seal-recovery area."

"We're going to see Sookie!" Meg cried.

Jen smiled at them and said, "I've been told

you three children were responsible for her rescue."

"Is she all better?" Meg asked.

"She certainly is," Jen said, as they followed her to a door behind the penguin habitat.

Jen led the small group down a hallway to the back of the aquarium where the building reached out into the harbor. They came to a large area where walls and a roof of glass enclosed a large pool of water. Two seals were lounging on the flat rocks that surrounded it.

"Which one is Sookie?" Luke asked.

"There she is!" Meg said, as a head popped up from the water.

"Would you like to feed her, Meg?" Jen asked.

"Oh, YES please!" Meg replied.

"It's feeding time, so you can all have a turn giving the seals a fish," Jen said.

Sookie swam over to a toy ball floating at one end of her swimming area. She dove under it and, using her nose, propelled it out of the water toward Kate.

Kate reacted quickly and caught the ball in her arms.

"Smile," Luke said, taking a picture of Kate in action.

"You're a clever girl, Sookie," Kate laughed.

"Are you training Sookie to be an entertainer at the aquarium?" asked Annie, as she carefully held a fish out to another seal named Milo.

"No, seals are just naturally playful," Jen said. "This area is for seal recovery. These seals are here because they were orphaned or injured. Our goal is to heal them and release them back in the wild—as close as possible to where we found them."

"So they can find their families?" Meg asked.

"Sookie's home is around Appledore Island," Luke said.

"Yes," Jen said. "We plan to free her there in the spring, so she can rejoin her group of harbor seals. The other two seals are gray seals, and they will be released near Cape Cod where they were found."

"Will you let us know when?" Kate asked.

"Maybe we can go out on Dad's boat and watch her being set free," Luke said.

"I'll let you know as soon as we confirm the date," Jen said.

After the visitors finished feeding the seals, everyone headed to the aquarium's exit.

"Hey, Meg," Luke said. "I saw you whisper something to Sookie. What did you tell her?"

"I told her to make sure she visited us at Creek Farm," Meg said with a smile. "She can find us by the fairy houses."

## Tracy Kane

Tracy Kane is the Author and Illustrator of the award winning Fairy Houses Series® of books and video.

Inspiration for the Series came when visiting an island off the coast of Maine. There she discovered small natural habitats hidden in the woods. What a great idea and activity to share with children...everywhere! And that was the magical moment that led to her first book, *Fairy Houses*.

Tracy has inspired many community groups to hold fairy houses events and spread the enchantment.

## Genevieve Aichele

Genevieve Aichele is the Artistic Director of New Hampshire Theatre Project in Portsmouth, NH and has performed, directed and taught theatre arts both nationally and internationally for over thirty five years. She has written numerous plays for both young people and adults, and published several books of poetry. This is her first novel (not counting the one she wrote at age 12) and she is honored to be a co-author with Tracy Kane.

# The Fairy Houses Series®

*Connecting Families and Nature...with a pinch of Fairy magic!*
*Winner of 12 Prestigious Awards*

## The Illustrated Series

(Ages 3 and up)

*New Release!*

### Fairy Houses Trilogy
#### by Tracy Kane

ISBN13: 978-0-9708104-3-4   $24.95
144 Pages  Softcover  11.25 x 8.75 in.

A collectors item containing all three illustrated stories from the award-winning Fairy Houses Series® - all in one book!

FAIRY HOUSES, FAIRY BOAT, and FAIRY FLIGHT books.

Enjoy the magic of Nature...building fairy houses!

*"Children's Book Sense" pick*
*American Booksellers Association*

---

### Fairy Houses
#### by Tracy Kane

ISBN10 0-9708104-5-8
ISBN13: 978-0-9708104-5-8

$15.95  40 Pages
Hardcover  11.25 x 8.75 in.

What happens if you build a house for the fairies to live in?

Will they come to visit?

*"Top 10 Pick" Children's Book Sense*
*American Booksellers Association*

---

### Kristen's Fairy House
UPC 884277000020
ISBN13: 978-09708104-9-6

$14.95   DVD 40 mins.

What is the mystery of the small habitats built in the woods by visiting children?

Join Kristen on a unique and wonderful adventure of discovery!

*Parents' Choice Gold Award Winner*
*As seen on National Public Television*